THE SEVEN
BRIDES-TO-BE
OF
GENERALISSIMO
VLAD

THE
SEVEN
BRIDES-TO-BE
OF
GENERALISSIMO VLAD

VICTORIA GODDARD

Underhill
Books

Grandview, PEI, 2016

First published in 2016 by Underhill Books in
Charlottetown, Prince Edward Island

ISBN: 978-0-9950270-5-3

Underhill Books
4183 Murray Harbour Drive
RR#3 Belfast PEI
CoA 1A0 Canada
www.underhillbooks.com

THE SEVEN BRIDES-TO-BE OF GENERALISSIMO VLAD

ONE • OVER RADFORD WAY

"No can do, I'm afraid, unless you've got something over Radford way."

"Radford! Whyever are you going there?"

"Wedding."

"People still get married? What is this, the 21st century? Portia, it's half a mill we're talking about."

I run a small, very fast, very exclusive sort of courier service. Nothing illegal, mind—but off-channels quite often. Giordano's never quite worked out how this works, but that's fine, he's just my official agent. He doesn't know about the other half of the business, either.

"I'm leaving on the second terminator," I added, to predictable squawking. I turned down the intercom when it became clear he had nothing else to add and set about preparing the ship for the cross-arm journey. I was going way past Radford, actually, past Arshen even, and I had to be ready for anything. Not just within reason: weird things happen in the debated spaces between stars.

Before you ask, I'm not much certain how the ship's engines work, either. In school we're told it's magic— way to encourage creative engineering, there, guys—and by the time I'd worked my way up the ranks in the merchant fleet I wasn't any closer to getting a handle on it from the scientists.

The other half of my business education suggested it *was* magic, with rather better logic.

"So who's getting married, anyway?"

I grinned at the intercom. Giordano couldn't see it, as I don't like visual communications when I'm flying, which is most of the time. Actually, I don't like viusual communications the rest of the time, the result of a bad accident that left me rather disfigured. Most of my acquaintances know me over the ether; they don't stare.

"My best friend from childhood," I responded to Giordano. "Fellow by the name of Vlad."

"Not the Vlad who just inherited the Generalship of Kinrod?"

It figured that Giordano would have heard. I sighed.

"Yep, the very same."

There was an impressed silence, or semi-silence, for Giordano tends to pant when he gets excited.

"Wow," he said eventually. "That's the society wedding of the year. Though isn't there something weird about how the Generalissimo has to pick his bride from a selection? Or marry seven women? One each from the First Families of Kinrod? I'm sure they were talking about it on the Galactic News …"

"It's nearly second terminator," I said, looking out the planetside porthole. The second sun of Laverhame was setting; the terminator line of night was coming underneath the fixed-point orbit of the space dock.

I finished off my last round of checks. "You didn't find anything for me?"

Giordano coughed, obviously retrieving his imagination from the seven brides-to-be of Generalissimo Vlad. "Just the Bethelain run—"

"Wrong direction."

"Even for half a mill?"

"Whatever. I promised Vlad I'd be at this wedding when I was ten, I'm not going the other direction and missing it for a piddly half mill."

"Must be nice to be rich."

"I just manage my money well. Anything else? I'm

about to head off."

"What are you getting the happy couple? Septuple?"

"He only has to marry one of them."

"I'm assuming if they're having an old-fashioned wedding, presents are expected."

"I haven't decided yet," I lied. "One of my origami pieces, I think, but I haven't decided which one."

"The Starblade Corkscrew is my favourite," he said, laughing.

We'd had this discussion before: it was modelled on that ship's engine, which was indeed shaped like a corkscrew. Giordano's hobby was a comparison taste of every wine grown in the extended human ecosystem of the northern galaxy. He felt this a pleasingly infinite hobby, more fun than my origami engines.

"Maybe I'll make a fleet," I said. "Talk to you when I'm back out this way."

"Bring me a bottle of Kinrodi champagne. I haven't tried it yet."

"I'll do my best."

I watched the luminous seas of Laverhame grow into their nighttime brilliance under me. The terminator line passed my marker buoy, and I started the ignition sequence while the station master went through the safety measures as if I hadn't ever left the double gravity well of a binary system before, instead of being one of the more frequent couriers to it. Ah well. I suppose I've only been doing this for ten years.

★★★

I was well on my way when my other agent contacted me.

Laverhame's two suns were a bright speck in the distance, well below me, Giordano's home of Beltong out of sight past the Crab Nebula, and I had finished two origami engines. This part of the route was one I flew six or eight times a year (Laverhame's a major hub of commerce for this entire section of the Eastern Arm), and I could handle the flunzes in my sleep. Which, obviously, I have to, given the distances involved.

Part of the magic of faster-than-light travel involves tracking on carefully selected lines of gravitational pull between stars, which some wag way back in early days had called *influenze*; over the years this contracted to flunzes.

The flunzes are easy to follow out on the arms, where there aren't so many stars exerting their own contradictory pulls. The skill comes in the denser parts of the galaxy, where most people live and most of the stars are. Also most of the ships, most of the renegades, most of the non-peaceful aliens, and most of the interstellar predators.

I was going towards Hasim's Star, and past there was the quickest way to Radford and Arshen beyond it, if one wishes to avoid the Star Nurseries.

One usually does wish to avoid the Star Nurseries.

I'm a good pilot, and my ship's one of the best, but I wanted a bit of down time to finish my origami wedding presents, so I was planning not to go straight through the centre of the galaxy but instead on a tight bend over it.

Of course, that was before the other agent called.

"Portia," he said quietly, and followed the spoken greeting with the musical key that scrambled my recorders and told me who was calling. Though after four years I recognized the three computer sims the agent used.

"Roger," I said. "En route to Arshen via Radford."

"On commission?"

Meaning, did I have a major run. "Not at the moment," I said, imagining my uncle Jack (who had gotten me into this side of the couriering) having fits on the other end. Not that he would want to go to the wedding, either. "Personal business."

Now, though—as I said—in my opinion this was the best way to Kinrod, it was not really on any of the normal shipping routes, or even the extended ones taught in the merchant navies of the Central League of Governments. My ship is something special, and I'm very good at navigating the flunzes.

But Arshen via Radford doesn't sound like it would go anywhere but the edge of the Star Nurseries.

"Can you pick up a passenger to courier?"

"Depends where said passenger is, and where to. I'd rather not."

"It's triple rate."

Passengers were already double my usual rate, since I prefer to fly alone, and my ship is very small. Triple my usual passenger rate—for any distance larger than a handful of parsecs—would take this well over Giordano's half mill territory.

"I'm listening," I said neutrally. Often the other agent and I enter into bantering, but he didn't seem inclined today, and I didn't want to get into details of where I was going just yet.

"I've a guest for the Millington wedding on Kinrod who's managed to strand himself at the Thimble on Singerman Prime."

"That's in the middle of the Star Nurseries!"

The agent ignored my incredulity with what I suspected was a grin, though even if I'd wanted to he certainly wouldn't have had visuals on. "Ask for Trev."

"Like there will be all that many people stranded on Singerman Prime," I muttered. "Any other instructions?"

"Don't be late for the wedding."

Even Uncle Jack—whatever role he had in that organization (higher than my agent, that was for sure)—wasn't to know I was definitely going to the wedding, so I swallowed "I wasn't intending to be," and managed, "Roger."

The other agent signed off with another musical key to unscramble my signals. I set the computer to access information about the Star Nurseries, Singerman Prime, and the Thimble, and turned to my charts to plot out a new route right through the centre of the galaxy.

Although I'm not at all suicidal—even when faced with a society wedding where my best friend from childhood has to choose between seven near-complete strangers bidding for a sudden jump in social status, *and* my entire extended family is invited—I can't say I was too annoyed at the prospect of having a legitimate reason to enter the region known to galactic rumour as the Road to Heaven, being at least as difficult as that infamous route.

TWO • DRINKS ON SINGERMAN PRIME

The way in was actually not too bad: the flunzes were tricky, but ten or fifteen other couriers might have made it. There were several solar sailfish, which are obviously not fish but do rather look like Earth manta rays, except on a suitably interstellar scale. Daredevils hunt them for the iridium and other precious elements in their skeletons and the helium in their air sacks, and for the photovoltaic scales on their wings.

I think they're a kind of plant, and photosynthesize. Then again I'm a courier, not a biologist, and my scientific interests are focussed on designing cool origami engines. It would annoy my mother that I don't know.

I'd seen two solar sailfish before in twelve years of

starfaring, the last four of which were the interesting years: I saw eighteen of the creatures after I passed the edge of the Habitable Zone and entered the Star Nurseries' Suburbs. The sailfish were sailing down the flunzes surrounded by small darting creatures I'd never seen before, not even in vids, and couldn't name. I took as many pictures as I could. I didn't want to annoy my mother *that* much.

The Star Nurseries is the dense heart of the galaxy clustered around the central black hole. Singerman is the artificial moon of an artificial planet set in a complex orbit around four stars just outside the event horizon of the black hole. No one knows who made it or why: an old-order alien species, obviously, but that's all. It's been moving slowly towards the black hole for billions of years, and right now is the closest anyone has ever gotten to the event horizon—well, and also come back.

The galactic encyclopedia told me all this, together with solemn warnings about how idiotic it was to try to go there. It also mentioned that the only thing that was definitely known to exist closer to the centre of the Road to Heaven was the Pearly Gates, a collapsed first-order former superstar.

One more-or-less sane astronomer had seen it from Singerman Prime, and spent the rest of his career attempting to account for what precise and delicate balance of forces could keep such a massive neutron star (as it was now) outside the black hole. One theory was that it was a magnet for dark energy.

I revised my opinion of the number of other couriers who could have been sent to fetch a passenger from there as I negotiated the approach to Singerman Prime: maybe seven.

The Thimble was not mentioned in the encyclopedia. I had to stop looking for information during the approach to the docks for fear of wrecking my ship and being stranded along with whatever idiot guest of Vlad's wedding was there. Along with the difficult flunzes Singerman's nearer orbits were full of crazily moving junk, the flotsam of the galaxy. It was probably a treasure trove to anyone willing to brave the radiation to investigate it.

There were three other ships in dock. Two were ancient, fifth-generation-Earth ships at the newest. They didn't look as if they'd moved since they got there. I guessed at least one of them belonged to a junk comber, though whether he (it was almost certainly a he) ever took his findings towards the civilized parts of the galaxy, and if so, how he got his ship to move, was a mystery.

Also a mystery was the third ship. It was a tiny fast vessel, the sort a very rich daredevil might own. I assumed it was "Trev's"—it had the look of belonging to some-one who'd be going to Generalissimo Vlad Millington's wedding—and the mystery wasn't in its looks so much as how anyone who would own one could possibly have gotten to Singerman Prime through the Star Nurseries.

And also why it was covered in score marks and singed flares.

Though that perhaps answered the need for a lift.

★★★

Inside the station I was obviously a stranger, but to-tally ignored. No one asked for identification; the pa-perwork was actual paper and really and truly asked for "name of use" and "preferred origin."

I filled in "Portia" and "Out and About" and the at-tendant, an alien from the Gasborlee Group, put it in a file (an actual physical file) without comment.

"The Thimble?" I asked, hesitantly.

"Fourth right," she rasped through the interpreter machine.

"Thanks," I said, and found the fourth right after fif-teen lifts and three flights of stairs.

The metal door had no sign, but it opened into a dim round room with a spiral staircase leading up. I climbed this, wondering about the whole place. Who came here?

Why? How? Where were their ships? What did they eat? Why did they have so very many stairs?—and eventually found myself, panting rather—space courier work doesn't generally involve a lot of climbing—in another dimly lit round room with a convex ceiling liberally dimpled.

The dimness came from the lack of artificial lights: the walls were some kind of plexiglas sheets open to the starfields, mostly occluded at the moment by Singerman Planet.

There were four people in the room, all male or equivalent. Two were Rigellan modified humans, one was a jumped-up dendroid from the Arshen system, and the fourth was my younger brother.

The dendroid seemed to be the bartender, or at least was the one to look up as I entered, so I ordered a local and plunked myself down next to "Trev." I guess it's easier to handle than Orion Mantrev Indoridoon McArthur XIV, a name passed down the boys of my family like a curse.

Trev didn't look up even when I sat down. He looked well plastered, in fact, though as I hadn't seen him in nearly a decade I suppose he might have looked that peaky as a regular thing.

I wondered who could possibly want him at the Millington wedding enough to pay three-quarters of a million credits for the joy.

"Trev?"

"Yeah."

The dendroid gave me a bowl of coffee. I raised my eyebrows: he did the tree equivalent of grinning, rustling all his leaves. A good friend of mine in the merchant naval academy was a dendroid, she had the most amazing way of blushing her leaves through three seasons when she felt excited.

"It's my specialty. Don't fret, it's got kick."

I was wondering where the coffee beans came from, actually, as synthesizers don't usually manage the esthers properly. It was spiced and laced with something that tasted like maple syrup but almost certainly wasn't. (Unless the dendroid was tapping himself? Perish that thought—please. I wish I hadn't had it.)

"Maybe a plain coffee for him?"

"Sure. What's the credit?"

"How about an origami bird?" I pulled out one of the sheets of best-quality gilt paper (gorgeous stuff in blue and gold patterns) I kept for the purpose, and under the delighted gaze of the dendroid created him a paper crane.

"That's worth more than two," he said, and swayed

off with the bird perched in his upper branches like a hair comb.

My brother took several tries to focus on me. He watched the paper-folding with a puzzled glance, went up to my face, winced, drank half his coffee when it arrived, and finally said, "Portia? What the hell are you doing here?"

"I heard you needed a lift, little bro. What happened to your ship? It looks like it was attacked by something."

"Portia, are you really here?"

I suppose it was a strange place for us to meet, far from the debutante's ball that had been my last family visit.

(I only went to that as a result of another promise to a childhood friend, that we'd stand together to be present-ed to Society—or at least that segment composed of the wealthy magnates who lived on Kinrod and Pangaia II. Charleen probably would have preferred it if I'd forgot-ten the promise. Certainly everyone else had.)

"Portia, how did you get here?"

"By spaceship. Yourself?"

He frowned mightily, took another huge swig of the coffee, and passed out.

I looked up at the dendroid. He waved his fronds helplessly. "It didn't have anything extra in it."

"How long has he been here?"

He rustles his branches. "A week? A year? Time's funny this close to the event horizon. He paid with gold coins of Kinrodel and came from farther in, babbling of green fields, and demanded drink."

I wondered if the dendroid read Shakespeare or if it was just the translator borrowing phrases to suit. Pressing matters were more that Trev was probably in some portion of the wedding party, if I knew anything about the Generalissimo's wedding (and Charleen, Vlad, and I had arranged enough of them as children to make us reasonable experts); and the dendroid was right—we were perilously close to the event horizon. I didn't want to spend any longer than I had to on Singerman Prime, strange and marvellous as the rest of the moon undoubtedly was.

I got one of the Rigellans to help me carry Trev to my ship. The station attendant watched incuriously, as if she'd been there for centuries and seen far stranger things. The stranger things were almost certain; the centuries were possible.

The daredevil ship was voice-locked as well as severely damaged to the point I wasn't sure how Trev had gotten out, and though it was smaller than my ship, it wasn't by much.

I thanked the Rigellan for his help, saw that the

station attendant was reading what looked like an actual physical book (another mystery, why someone had brought it all the way there when every ounce of extra gravitational mass matters, that close to the event horizon), and paying no attention to me at all.

My ship looks like one of the Firedance range of fast couriers, the model from about five years ago. And so its main body is. It has a number of modifications, however, some arranged for by the other agency, and some of them by me. One of these is that it has an implication hold.

Don't fret that you've never heard of this. Mine was one of the first, possibly the very first, come through Uncle Jack's efforts at the agency, unless I much miss my mark.

An implication hold disentangles molecular bonds — more creative engineering mysticism, I know—basically it permits two objects to share one space. Well, not really one space, as that is impossible except possibly for electrons; but as every kid knows, most of anything material is empty space. My ship's hold is space specially made to let its empty space be taken up by another object's atoms.

You can believe that didn't come cheap – and you'd better believe that very few people know I have it. It's not even classified. It doesn't officially exist.

I buckled Trev into the sleeping couch, did my preflight checks, and got bored permission to leave.

The attendant hadn't asked what I was doing with the unconscious Trev, didn't ask why I was taking his ship, why I'd come or why I was leaving after not even a standard hour on dock. She didn't even ask me for docking fees. It was both refreshingly simple and utterly terrifying at the same time. It was pretty clear I could have done anything I wanted to do on Singerman Prime.

I guess law and order stand as little chance as physical reality this close to event horizon.

The Thimble on Singerman Prime is the closest artifical object to the centre of the galaxy. Or it was, until the double mass of my ship and my brother's slipped between two flunzes and got caught by one leading directly to the black hole.

THREE • AT THE PEARLY GATES

It was totally my own fault. I was looking backwards at the Thimble, trying to figure out what else the structure reminded me of, simultaneously imagining a new origami engine that made use of some of its elegant and strange protuberances, and jumped when I glanced forward again to see a very strange interstellar creature looming to my port side.

I dropped down and starboard immediately, had to swerve out of the path of the ruin of a truly ancient alien ship, and since I'd already started the flunze access sequence, was easily caught by the strongest flunze of them all.

Focus, Portia, I thought to myself. Your brother's on

the ship.

Some people find an uprush of tenderness when they're responsible for a sleeping relative or friend. They feel protective, strong, in charge. They want to treat the person as gently as a work of art, cradled in their love, that sort of sentimental gloop.

I'm not a very sentimental person. I was just grateful that Trev was unconscious and wasn't there to witness my failure to chart an elegant course. My current one looked like instructions for an origami engine.

My mind is annoying that way, the more I should be focussed on something else the more creative ideas it comes up with. I kept seeing the shape of Singerman Prime and the strange tentacles of the interstellar creature that was totally gliding down the flunzes after me, and thinking up engines.

All right, I thought.

I was caught in the natural equivalent of a tractor beam, the gravitational pull of the galactic black hole. I was perilously close to the event horizon. I was being followed by a very large and very mysterious tentacled creature that seems perfectly at home in the Star Nurseries.

I was seriously going to be late for Generalissimo Vlad's wedding.

Oh, no, you don't get me that way, I swore to nothing

in particular. I'd spent too long building my reputation.

I'd never broken a promise, not one, not even that stupid one to stand next to Charleen at the debutante ball when we were presented to the former Generalissimo (Vlad's uncle Ilya Ivonovich). That was just after the accident at the Merchant Navy Academy that left me disfigured beyond the skill of galactic cosmetic surgery, and the response of Society had not been kind. But Vlad had danced with me.

Like hell was I going to be sucked into the black hole and break a promise to *him*.

I took several deep breaths. Looked out the various windows and at the even more various screens, which showed me visions of the galaxy in media ranging from gamma waves to gravity.

After a bit I turned off everything but the visible spectrum and the gravitational model. The interstellar predator was a big black and purple shape in the visible-spectrum monitors. It looked like something H.P. Lovecraft had made up, and the part of my mind that was not seriously annoyed was gibbering with fear.

In the gravitational simulation it was a superbly beautiful creature that could revolutionize my origami if I just had five minutes to watch it properly and a lifetime to use the lessons of its curvatures and mass pockets. It seemed to be able to manipulate where the mass lay in its body so that it could move in the gravitational fields as easily as a bird soared through planetary air.

I got the five minutes, though given how far into the centre of the galaxy we were our relative time probably didn't equate to anyone else's. I watched it follow us lazily, coming closer without apparent effort.

In the visible spectrum its tail swished idly back and forth. In the gravitational imaging its mass shifted and sent out ripples into the ether.

I knew my engine intimately. My gravitational signature was rather different than usual because of my brother's ship, which was not like a usual cargo, in that it had something in it that was not properly anchored. Its weight kept shifting my ship's centre of gravity.

I realized that the predator was anchoring its mass further and further to the upward starboard side, as if it were counterbalancing some sort of new pull that hadn't yet come into my awareness. I studied the flunzes. They were exceptionally close together, making it very difficult to read them and even more difficult to plot a course, especially as the pull of the black hole overwhelmed pretty much the entire gravitational efforts of the rest of the galaxy.

Pretty much being the key phrase, there.

The predator didn't seem to mind the event horizon at all. Unless it existed only moving relative to the centre? Could a creature exist in only one spatial dimension, the way human beings exist in one temporal one? Could it move in multiple temporal dimensions? Was it *made* of antimatter?

Were there even multiple temporal dimensions in the most recent physical theories?

After an infinite period of time, I thought that it didn't matter what the theories said, it mattered what the universe *was*.

But no—I'd seen the creature move sideways into my space. And its tail, or whatever it was, was going up and down, so clearly it did move in at least three spatial dimensions. It wasn't moving only towards the black hole. But how was the predator moving *across* the flunzes? How did it go *away*?

There was too much information on the gravitational screen to decipher the important data. After a bit of creative banging on the settings keys I eventually managed to dim the strength of the centripetal gravitational force and could see the weak reciprocal forces of the rest of the universe.

The only other stable object between Singerman Prime and the centre of the galaxy, so the encyclopedias had said, was a collapsed supernova that was currently poised at the exact centre of pull between Singerman Planet, three of the first-order neutron stars that had collapsed in the first wave of galactic creation, and the black hole.

Or, you know, it was the bridgehead of Hell, if the other name of the Pearly Gates was correct.

My saviour.

There it was. A thirteen-billion year old dead star, caught in a gravitational eddy, something a few crazy astrophysicists who had gotten as far as Singerman Prime had once seen. A dead star, *not* directly ahead of me. A neutron star, dense enough, if I got the angles right, if I caught the moment, to deflect me from my course.

It was the most difficult and dangerous piece of flying I have ever done, requiring the most focus, the most delicate touch, the most split-second timing. Of course, this is why I nearly killed my brother four different ways when he said, "Aargh, Cthulu is following us!" right in my ear.

I jerked violently away from him, which meant I yanked the controls out of their precise configuration and sent us plunging relentlessly toward's the neutron star's gravity well.

Trev sat back hastily. I blanked out all distractions.

What was left in the now were the two disastrously strong flunzes of the Pearly Gates now directly ahead (in space terms) and the black hole off towards the upper right, and the now anxiously spiralling movements of the space monster.

Seeing its obvious tentacle-twitching anxiety set my own into extreme panic mode. I worked the flunzes futilely—nothing deflected us from the fast-approaching neutron star.

Not only was I going to miss the wedding, I wouldn't even get to find out if there really was a wormhole across time in the centre of the galaxy.

The predator was going back and forth across the flunzes but not following us on our precipitous fall forward. I was distractingly amazed by its beauty, by its ability to cross the flunzes, to balance gravitational forces by manipulating its own mass—for all I knew it was doing something with the weak nuclear force, too, like my implication hold.

I wished there was a way I could manipulate my own ship's mass, but there wasn't much I could do besides jettison Trev's ship and its ill-balanced cargo, and that was hardly going to help much.

—Except that in the moment of reconfiguration I might be able to reconnect to the galactic flunze, or even better Singerman Prime's—and maybe—

I heaved a somewhat blasphemous prayer to my mother's gods and pressed the hold release sequence.

There is a well-known phenomenon whereby the mind dilates time when space gets overly crowded. My older sister Camilla studies these things; she used me as a case study once.

This is what happened.

Halfway through the release sequence, the weight in Trev's ship swung like a compass needle to point to the central black hole. His ship thereupon slewed round, which caused it to jam in my hold door—which is not part of the implication folds—and my ship started to wobble.

I have never seen anything organic move so fast as the predator. One tentacle was in and around Trev's ship before I had finished processing the wobble.

In a burst of inspiration I hit the emergency override closure.

The predator made an electronic flare that shrieked through my ship's speakers like a banshee caught in static. It then pulsed its mass from near-void to neutron-star density too quickly to get more than the impression that that was what it was doing. The trapped tentacle made an unholy thumping noise in the implication hold.

But it got itself, somehow, into a neutral balance be-tween the flunzes. Since it was still caught in my hold, this meant that I was, too, a result that more than made up for the fact that it then started to attack me.

I watched it cycle through two attacks with another prayer that my ship would still be able to fly afterwards. It was almost acting like a bellows, if its medium was gravity instead of air—it ballooned its tentacles out in space while it pulsed lighter and lighter, then contracted both body and mass to wallop my ship like the hammer of Thor.

On a nerve-edge of reaction I waited through the third period of expansion to what I judged just the mo-ment before its greatest extent, and on that moment I released its tentacle, and blessed Newton's third law as the reaction let me take action—the abrupt change in the gravitational fields around us as our combined masses separated let me get my ship the hell out of there.

FOUR • INTERSTELLAR SQUID

Ten minutes later, if ten minutes means anything, I was coasting sideways around the galactic hub and picking up flunzes leading every-which-way as if they were pieces of gold someone had dropped between the stars. Each star's gravitational well was an oasis, each one promising a way out, a haven, a place of safety. It didn't matter that most of them were entirely hostile to all life, and half the rest hostile to human life. They were not the black hole, and that was by far enough.

I then turned to my brother, who was sitting on the other chair with his hands gripping each other hard enough to go numb. "Don't ever interrupt me when I am negotiating the flunzes again."

His eyes were wide. "We just missed crashing into a neutron star."

"Correct. We also just missed the event horizon of the galactic black hole. What the hell do you have in your ship?"

"The *event* horizon?"

"I just picked you up from Singerman Prime. That neutron star was the Pearly Gates."

"Oh God."

"And yes, in answer to your earlier statement, Cthulu's interstellar cousin is following us. Since you seemed to recognize it, and since your ship seems to have been attacked by it, what have you got that it wants so badly to follow us out of the Star Nurseries?"

"Oh God."

"We're coming close to the Habitable Zone. Come on, little bro, if you want to get to the Millington wedding on time—"

"Oh God."

A thought struck me. "Is it your wedding present?"

Trev turned a slightly different horrified expression on me. "What?"

"Your present. You know, for Vlad's wedding."

My brother unstuck his fingers from each other with obvious difficulty so he could run his hands through his hair in a distraught fashion. I let him sort himself out while I caught one of the blessedly normal, familiar, only slightly dangerous flunzes, and let the ship move into its smooth semi-automatic mode.

Trev's voice was a good imitation of our mother's when she was being very patient.

"I went all the way into the Road to Heaven so that I didn't have to go to that wedding. I took a commission from Uncle Jack to go looking for the Old Ones so that I didn't have to go to that wedding. I drank something awful a *tree* made for me so I didn't have to go to that wedding."

I grinned; it's nice being a big sister sometimes. "Well, someone wants you there enough to pay me three times my usual passenger rate, little bro."

"I would have thought *you'd* make any excuse to avoid going to the society wedding of the year."

I shrugged. "So what is in your ship's hold that this monster wants so badly?"

He looked at my screens; I'd put on the usual range, infrared, gamma rays, visual, gravitational, the whole she-bang. The tentacled predator floated along as easily behind us as if we hadn't just had nearly been sucked in by a black hole.

"I think I might have found its egg."

★★★

The Interstellar Millington Squid (hey, we were the first ones to report it, we got to name it) followed us along the flunzes past Arshen and Dreamhaven and the Wavery Lightfields. It didn't seem inclined to attack us, and as I didn't have any weapons—again, I might run under-the-table things around the galaxy, but I don't do anything *illegal*—I decided to go on as usual.

Admittedly I don't usually have a relative on board, nor do I usually spend quite so much time looking over my shoulder.

After I put the ship in normal mode, I made food for us in the ship's galley. Trev looked as if he'd remembered that he had a hangover, and although I was tempted to let him suffer a while longer I eventually gave him medicine to stop his whining. He watched me do some domestic things, cooking, tidying, rearranging the main area of the ship.

It's not a very big ship. My main area is about the size of a goodly planetside apartment, open-plan so I can see what the screens are doing from the couches or table. I have a separate bedchamber up above, but pretty well only use it when I'm docked somewhere. One of the reasons I have more money than Giordano is that I don't own property anywhere else except as investments.

Over pad thai Trev said, "As I was going through the Navy, people kept asking me if I was as good a pilot as you. Can you fly like your sister, they said. Over and over again. Are you going to be a courier like her."

"And are you?" I asked, when he didn't add anything else.

He pushed around his noodles. "I couldn't fly like you—I can't believe you didn't crash on the Pearly Gates. That was amazing flying."

I shrugged, but I was pretty pleased, really. Not at nearly crashing, but at the fact that we got out of that alive. "I'll be happier once we get to Kinrod and get this farce over with. Not to mention get rid of our friend yonder. Though possibly Mother would like to study it."

"Are you really making me go to this wedding?"

"You bet. I'm not going to lose three quarters of a mill because you don't want to get dressed up."

He grinned reluctantly. "What are you going to give them, then?"

I showed him my little fleet of origami engines. I had twelve left from previous travels, plus the ones I'd been working on since, and they made an impressive display, if I do say so myself, on the niches along the walls from the bridge to the galley.

Trev picked up the Corkscrew Starblade. He had gentle hands, I was glad to see, and ran his fingers lightly over the folds.

"You look puzzled," I said, equally lightly. "That's a Corkscrew Starblade."

"Third model," he agreed. "Is this paper? They have circuit designs drawn on them."

"I like them to be accurate."

"They're beautiful. A Jasmine Starblade IV, and what are these? They look like variations on the Firedance New Series, but I've not seen them in any of the catalogues."

"Sometimes I get creative."

He looked thoughtful. "Do you think I could make something for the Generalissimo? I really don't have anything."

We MacArthurs are known for our art, but I couldn't think what Trev's interests were—drinking, I'd thought.

"You've got a new species and its egg," I said. "Those are all yours, little bro. I'm going to make a few more origami pieces based on what I saw along the Road to Heaven. You amuse yourself. I've got the *Complete Works of Mark Twain* upstairs, if you want a book."

"An actual physical book?"

"Fifteen of them, as it happens. Electronics get a little

funny when you're out on the Edge. Or in the Centre, as I can now attest with certainty."

"So it's true."

"What is?"

He set down the Corkscrew Starblade in its spot. "That you courier the whole galaxy."

"That's where the fun is."

"And the money?"

I grinned. "That too. Come on, we've got a week to Kinrod. Even you can read *The Celebrated Jumping Frog of Calaveras County* in a week."

"Can't wait."

★★★

The other agent contacted me when I was sliding down from Valrei's gravitational orbit onto the last of the flunzes. Kinrodel Star was becoming a noticeably bright spot, and I had about half an hour before getting clearances, and another hour of deacceleration after that before I had to concentrate on the final approach.

The musical chime sounded. Trev was upstairs asleep on my bed (something confirmed by the ship's sensors), but I made sure the door was closed securely before answering. "Portia here."

"Job status?"

"Parcel retrieved."

The agent laughed. He was using the female sim today, but though the laughter came at an appropriate register its rhythm was the same across all three sims. "Any problems?"

"The parcel brought a friend back from the Pearly Gates. Name of Peter."

I toggled the switch to send a picture of the interstellar squid. I was rewarded by the most pregnant silence I'd ever received from the intercom. It was even more fraught than when I told my mother I couldn't attend my oldest sister's first baby's christening because I was helping start a war in the Eastern Arm.

"What the hell is that?"

"Trev and I have decided that it's the Interstellar Millington Squid. He thinks it's following its egg, which is in his ship."

"Why is—you've got his ship in the implication hold."

"Roger that. However, his ship was attacked while in dock at Singerman Prime" (that had taken him a while to explain, since I'd had to ask delicately without explaining why exactly I had an implication hold, or what it was), "and he could barely get out a window. It'll need special equipment to open the hull."

"Right," said the agent, sounding the most distracted I'd ever heard him be. "Uh ... did you say it's the Millington Squid?"

"It has the most *amazing* manipulation skills."

Another pregnant silence. "Will you release Trev's ship to the care of the South Moon folks? They'll give the following passcode."

"Roger that," I said cheerfully. I recorded the musical key as given and set the implication hold to release only after. "I should note that Trev wishes to give the egg and the creature to the Generalissimo as his wedding present."

I was on fire today; the third pregnant silence was even better.

I chuckled to myself when the agent merely said, "We'll be in touch about your next assignment," with studied blandness, and set my new course to get round the backside of Kinrod's second moon.

Trev didn't ask about my routing, just how long we had till the wedding. "About two hours after landing," I said, having found this out when I talked to Kinrod Central about docking, and incidentally put through a call to Charleen, who wasn't there to take it.

My brother made an appalled face. "What the hell am I going to wear?"

"Call for a transporter," I suggested. "Get Camilla or

someone to send your kit with the driver."

"You're so sensible, Portia, I don't know how anyone can stand it. What about you? What are you wearing?"

"Not having crashed my ship, I brought my outfit with me. You use the shower first while I see us docked."

He took long enough in the shower (well, it's not water, but that's close enough) that I managed to offload his ship to the South Moon and get us in line for Kinrod Central Station before he came down.

I was deeply relieved that the Interstellar Squid followed the damaged ship and not us, as bringing a major predator any closer to planetary orbit wasn't going to win me any friends.

After I docked, while the ship was going through de-contamination coupling, I showered and dressed quickly in my own outfit. I'd bought it ages ago, when the wedding was announced, along with the special chest for my origami engines. Seventeen engines, nine of them of my own design, in a metal and glass case on anti-grav floats.

Trev had managed to arrange the transporter success-fully, and it did indeed have his formal wear aboard. He put on the old-fashioned coat and trousers resentfully.

"These were in style five hundred years ago," he mut-tered. "You'd think they'd come up with something new."

Personally I quite liked the women's style, probably

because I don't have to wear it every day. Long skirts and shapely bodices can be flattering, though, and I do have a reasonable figure.

And nice curly brown hair, too, not that anyone ever notices it.

FIVE • THE WEDDING PRESENT

Giordano had been quite right that there were some strange aspects to the wedding of the Generalissimo of Kinrod, and that this involved, somehow, the choice of seven brides.

As I understood it, years and years ago when Kinrod was first settled, there were eight major families. Organized crime syndicates from old Earth, some people said, but that's not recorded (obviously) in the family history books.

What is recorded is that two of the first Kinrodi-born children tried to get married to each other. Not a problem, except that their families were ancient and long-standing enemies, and after much to-ing and fro-ing a planetary war erupted.

This is why we now read Shakespeare in Kinrodi schools.

After a period the Millingtons came out on top, and established the Generalship to rule the rest. There remained a need to work out alliances without creating more rancour, and so someone had the bright idea that each new Generalissimo, on inheriting, would marry one of the appropriate generation (and gender) from the other families.

But of course, the question immediately became, which one?

Generalissima Natassja Petrovna Millington the First decided in her wisdom that what was needed was a way to make alliances without enemies. The only way to do this, she reasoned, was to make sure that each new Generalissimo picked a bride from one of the other families at random.

But how to make it truly random?

A blind ballot, was suggested by someone. Someone else came up with the idea that it should be done in person, so each of the potential spouses would wear thick veils.

After a few generations the Millingtons, having chosen some very strong spouses with very strong families, ended up dwindling as the dictators of Kinrod and Pangaia II, and instead ended up the figurehead leaders of a Syndicate made up of all eight Families, usually spending the majority of their time doing some sort of other job.

The tradition of the choice of seven brides continued, but now was made a choice between dowries. Each bride-(or groom)-to-be is dressed in a full veil and presents the Generalissimo with a gift that is supposed to represent her personality and charms (and only incidentally her family's wealth), and he picks from among them.

When Vlad's cousin Aleksandra Ilyinichna died when we were ten and he realized he'd inherit the Generalship, he made me promise, on all solemn vows, that I would ensure I was the MacArthur option when he inherited.

While Trev changed in one half of the transporter, Charleen called back. She said, "Portia. You weren't joking, then?"

"Nice to hear from you, too, Charleen. How are things?"

"The ceremony is in *one hour*. Where are you?"

I looked out the window. "Uh, half an hour away?"

She sighed. "You're lucky beyond measure that Katya is in love with a Lucano and doesn't mind you taking her place. Your mother is going to kill you, however."

It wasn't so much luck; it was obvious that my cousin Katya was gay from about the age of four. The other MacArthurs of my generation are all boys, except for my older two sisters, and Camilla was married and Imogen engaged when Aleksandra Ilyinichna died and the gender dynamic for the next Generalissimo shifted abruptly.

"I promised Vlad."

"Generalissimo Vladimir Grigorevich."

"Whatever. Where should I meet you?"

She sighed again. "Katya and I are in the upstairs powder room."

I heard a noise, looked back. "Trev's coming out, I'd better go. See you shortly!"

"You're only that cheerful because no one knows you're coming."

★★★

I made Trev promise, with many strong and solemn oaths, that he would not on any account tell anyone I was there, and guessed he might keep quiet for a full ten minutes, if that.

(In this I wronged him, as it turned out: he didn't tell anyone for half an hour, mostly because he was shanghaied on entering to form part of the Generalissimo's entourage, and was too busy cracking rude jokes to discuss sisters.)

I'd brought a coat, as it was autumn in this part of Kinrod, and since the fates were with me it was raining and I could legitimately have the hood up for the dash between the transporter and the building where the ceremony was held. I realized it had been months since the last time I was planetside; it was a bit of a strange feeling to have real air and real gravity and real rain.

The surrealism didn't go away when I went in. I was too young to remember the last Choosing Ceremony, but the decorations were the same as the annual Syndicate Meetings or the Debutantes' Ball. The clashing colours of the eight Families, hordes of people, extended relatives crying insincere and overly-sincere greetings to people they saw as little as possible, waitstaff eeling through the crowds—the normal run of things for a society function, and about as far away from the life of a solitary galactic courier as could be.

The second powder room upstairs was reserved for the MacArthur Bride. I ducked in just as the next door along started to open, hoping desperately the Lucano party wouldn't see me go in.

Charleen and Katya were sitting inside. Their skirts were several feet fuller than mine, hoop skirts apparently having come back into fashion in the months between the announcement and the ceremony. The tailors

I'd hired had done their best with my descriptions and Kinrodi fashion magazines, but my gown's style had a definite Central Galactic flair to its skirts.

They looked up at my entrance. Charleen frowned.

"You look wonderful, Katya," I said, meaning it. I hadn't seen her since the ill-fated debutante's ball, when she was fourteen and gawky. The ten years since had filled her out, but the bigger change was in her sparkling eyes and confident smile.

"You look just the same, Portia," said Charleen, but that probably was the case.

Katya worried at her gloves. "Are you sure you want to take my place? The Family is going to flip out."

"I promised Vlad I'd give him the option."

Charleen looked at me quizzically. "When was the last time you saw him?"

"I haven't been home since we debuted."

Katya made a face of surprise. Charleen, ever my sensible, conventional friend (and safely married to a most delightful young man of the Wong clan, and therefore not required to be the Armstrong representative at the ceremony), sighed again.

"He's changed quite a bit since then, especially since he stopped having to answer to anyone. Wild rides, crazy parties, disappearing off to the back of beyond …"

"A promise is a promise," I said, firmly, squashing the impulse to explain the charms of the back of beyond to those who hated leaving planetside. "Come on, the ceremony must be about to start. I don't want to be late."

They didn't argue, just set about helping me arrange the voluminous folds of the white veil across myself.

After we finished, Katya said tentatively, "I've got my dower chest here."

I looked at her wedding present. She'd obviously tried. It was a beautiful wooden box, elegantly carved, lined with red velvet, and filled with gems of glittering splendour. There were New Fabergé trinkets and delicate clockwork mechanisms, which represented her own not inconsiderable artistic skills. Like her, it was a wealth of beauty and joyous craft.

"Thank you," I said, not missing Charleen's head-shake; as a representation of my personality it was about as appropriate as a horse. "I brought my own wedding present, though."

Katya looked relieved. Before I could make an excuse not to open the lid of my chest, a bell rang sonorously from down below, and we heard doors opening and shutting all along the hall.

Charleen said, "It's time," and Katya, "We can still switch places," and I, "I flew all the way from the Eastern

Arm for this, I'm not backing out now. Come on, ladies, let's see whom Generalissimo Vlad chooses from his seven brides-to-be."

★★★

Downstairs the room was sweltering and appallingly full of people, most of whom I only vaguely recognized. Charleen was my attendant; Katya slipped off to stand with her Lucano girlfriend Venezia, out of the way of suspicious MacArthur eyes.

We were in the middle of the group of veiled women. We milled around for a few moments before lining up at one side of the room. The tradition was for the Generalissimo to come in with six companions to inspect the dower chests.

The companions aren't required to marry the other six women, by the way, but just to partner with them in the dances that follow the Generalissimo's choice and the wedding.

I found myself at the far end from the door, last in line. I was quite close to some members of my own family, Uncle Jack prominent among them. He was dressed in the formal uniform of the Syndicate, with lots of medals of honour. As the Syndicate's Chief of Intelligence he was given the task of making the first, formal inspection of the dowries, which became wedding presents for those who weren't chosen. Theoretically he could reject one of the chests as unsatisfactory, though in practice that had only happened once.

That was another Shakespearean period of Kinrodi history, though instead of *Romeo and Juliet* it was rather more *Titus Andronicus*.

Uncle Jack paced along the dais, nodding gravely at each of the chests. When he came to mine he looked down at the seventeen origami engines, nodded, paused, looked twice at the chest, flickered a glance up at me, then went off again with a suspiciously straight face to announce that all the gift-offerings were satisfactory and that the Generalissimo and his entourage could come in.

My heart was beating rather fast, which was stupid of it. I hadn't felt so much apprehension when nearly crashing on the Pearly Gates—probably because I had had something to do rather than stand there looking pretty, which, as you may have gathered, is not my usual *modus operandi*. Besides, my ship has far better climate control than any planetside building.

I was supposed to face forward, but when the Generalissimo came in surrounded by a pack of leaping puppies —sorry, young men of rank and station and good clothing—I turned my head very slightly so I could see him through the weave of the cloth.

He had changed, as Charleen had said, from the serious young man of one-and-twenty who had remembered his promise to dance with me at the debutante ball, no matter what his uncle said. He looked now like a rich young rake, a daredevil, a fop. His outfit was dashing, his expression was sardonic, his hair was overly done up.

I wondered how big of a mistake I'd made. But there was nothing for it, and as he had kept that long-ago promise, so would I keep mine. I wasn't going to let him *win*.

So I straightened my back, smiled under the veil, folded my hands politely as I'd been taught in long-ago deportment lessons, and waited.

He smiled charmingly to each of the veiled women, admired their offerings, displayed choice objects to the assembled Families, spoke cheerful nothings so that they giggled attractively behind their veils.

Gold, gems, precious substances from Kinrod and Pangaia and the rest of the galaxy. An heirloom dagger in a box of silk and tea—there, I thought, was someone being very honest about her character; I was surprised Katya hadn't thought of it. A chest full of seeds, promise of fruitfulness and love of the land. Feathers and ivory, singing crystals of Rigel, a tiara.

A very plain metal and glass chest with wooden shelves and lighting, and seventeen origami models of spaceship engines made out of a special sort of paper.

Generalissimo Vladimir Grigorevich Millington stood for a good minute before my chest in obvious utter consternation.

The six companions (one of whom was my brother Trev, looking equally utterly appalled) crowded about him, making ribald comments loud enough for me to hear but not for the matriarchs and patriarchs in the assembly behind them. I smiled with stiff cheeks even under the veil, feeling the tug of the scarring. This was going to be as bad as the debutantes' ball.

Then, without looking at me (well, at the veil), or saying anything, the Generalissimo turned and went to the announcement podium.

He said, and I didn't recognize his voice at all, which was mildy terrifying, "I have been told that the dowry chests of each of the ladies here present have been of their own choice, to represent her character and her promise to me. I have examined them carefully. Six of the seven are beautiful, rich, splendid, promising me joys as limitless as the diamonds of the Wong family, as rich as the wines of South Kinrodel, as to the point as the Lucano heritage. I am humbled by their offerings."

He paused. You could see that everyone was wondering what the MacArthur clan had wrought.

(It's always the MacArthurs, in these cases.)

People glanced sharply at each other as the Five MacArthur Sisters tried to figure out how far off the wall Katya had gone. I could see my mother glaring at Trev, as if it were his fault. He was gazing piteously at me. I couldn't see Uncle Jack.

The Generalissimo took a deep breath. "One of the seven has provided me with work of her own hands. An ancient art, folding paper. Nothing much, you'd think, except—" He broke down, looked back across at me, with an expression of—well, it was still consternated. I closed my eyes.

"Nineteen years ago I found out that my cousin Aleksandra Ilyinichna had died, and that I would therefore inherit the Generalship of Kinrod. Being ten years old, the prospect of the seven brides terrified me, and I made my closest friend at the time, Portia McGallagher MacArthur, promise that she would be the MacArthur Bride at my choosing ceremony."

There was a definite stir in the crowd when he said that. People looked suspiciously at me, then at my mother. She looked both baffled and furious.

Vlad said, "We made a pact that the way I would

know her would be that she would bring me a fleet of spaceships."

Half the room burst out laughing. Vlad put up his hand for silence. "I know, it is quite obvious that the dowry chests do not contain seventeen ships—that was how big we'd decided a fleet ought to be. I don't remember what our logic was; it might have had something to do with how many horses my father had at the time."

He smiled. "The dower chests contain treasures of Kinrod and from across the galaxy, to show me what I might choose, and choose well, and be happy choosing."

Well, it's a hard line to walk between statesmanship and being a rake, I guess.

"Most people in this room remember what happened at the Debutantes' Ball when Portia McGallagher MacArthur was presented to my uncle and was shamed before the assembly. She has not come to any of the Syndicate functions since, and I think we all understand why."

Or being a prat.

"I only bring this up because I want everyone here to understand that I choose a woman of courage, of fortitude, of honour. She is probably the greatest courier alive, and she brought me seventeen origami ship's engines as her dowry."

And he laughed, as at a private joke, and I melted

with relief that I hadn't been a total and complete fool, for just as I'd recognized it through three different computer sims, I recognized it now.

★★★

Later that evening, Uncle Jack found me.

"Six of those are new designs," he said, accusingly.

I smiled. "Have you seen what Trev got us?"

Uncle Jack sipped his wine with an aggrieved expression. "I shipped him off to the Star Nurseries' Suburbs to get him out of your mother's hair, and what happens? He ends up in the Road to Heaven and nearly kills you."

"Well, better than him staying in the Thimble until it gets sucked into the black hole."

There was a little pause. We watched people dancing, and Vlad talking to the six potential brides-not-to-be. Then Uncle Jack murmured, "You had the dress and the engines made long before Vlad sent you to pick up your brother."

I grinned at him. Maybe later I'd explain the flaw in the computer sim, the long years of bantering, the flirting over the ether, but for the moment that was my own secret.

★★★

Later that night, apropos of nothing we were doing, Generalissimo Vlad said, "The Interstellar Millington Squid, really?"

"All those games of space exploration and superheroes we used to play ..."

"I seem to recall ... No. I've just remembered something from that game. Please don't—no, better yet—*Promise* me you won't make me call our firstborn MacArtful MacArthur the Sly."

I laughed. "I promise."

The Seven Brides-to-Be of Generalissimo Vlad is something of an anomaly among my stories, as it is not connected to any of the rest (which are part of a sprawling narrative universe and firmly on the fantastical end of the speculative fiction spectrum).

One year I walked down the length of England, an activity rather befitting the medievalist-turned-fantasy novelist. I took a break in the middle of this journey to go to Florida for a friend's wedding, an option obviously not available to hobbits. On the plane ride across the Atlantic I was reflecting on the distance I was travelling, and I fell to wondering just how far someone might be willing to go. Across the ocean? Across the world? Across the galaxy? Such was the inspiration for Portia's voyage.

Shakespeare makes frequent appearances in my first novel, *Till Human Voices Wake Us*, which is a retelling of the myth of Orpheus and Eurydice set in a mostly-real modern London. *Stargazy Pie*, book one of Greenwing & Dart, is a comedy of manners set in a secondary world something of a cross between post-fall-of-Rome Europe and Regency England. Three other novellas, *The Tower at the Edge of the World*, *The Bride of the Blue Wind,* and *Victi Magnificamur* begin the tales of the Red Company, adventures for those who like a little philosophy with their swashbuckling.